For Henry and Nina, whom I love like my own.
So glad to be one of your bobs! —L.G.S.

For my favorite drippy babies:
Sam, Jack, Ben, Jeremy, and Sophie —A.V.

To Kevin Lewis. Thank you, my friend, for the laughs,
the love, and the "booger green" —M.C.

First Edition, February 2017
10 9 8 7 6 5 4 3 2 1
FAC-029191-16323
Printed in Malaysia

Library of Congress Cataloging-in-Publication Data
Names: Vernick, Audrey, author. | Scanlon, Elizabeth Garton, author. |
Cordell, Matthew, 1975- illustrator.
Title: Bob, not Bob! / by Audrey Vernick and Liz Garton Scanlon ; illustrated
by Matthew Cordell.
Description: First edition. | Los Angeles New York : Disney-Hyperion, [2017] |
Summary: "When a young boy gets a cold, he just wants his mommy. But his
stuffy nose makes it difficult for him to call out to his mom—not 'Bob,'
who happens to be the family dog"—Provided by publisher.
Identifiers: LCCN 2015033354 | ISBN 9781484723029 (hardcover)
Subjects: | CYAC: Cold (Disease)—Fiction. | Sick—Fiction. | Mother and
Child—Fiction. | Humorous stories.
Classification: LCC PZ7.V5973 Bm 2017 | DDC [E]—dc23
LC record available at http://lccn.loc.gov/2015033354

Reinforced binding

Visit www.DisneyBooks.com

To be read as though you have the worst cold ever:

BOB, NOT BOB!

written by **Liz Garton Scanlon** & **Audrey Vernick**
pictures by **Matthew Cordell**

𝔇𝔦𝔰𝔫𝔢𝔭 · HYPERION

Los Angeles   New York

Little Louie wasn't all that little.
It wasn't like he needed his mom
every minute of the day.

Usually.

But when Little Louie got sick, he felt littler than usual.

Tick Tock Tick

Like maybe his mom should check on him kind of often.
(Every three minutes or so.)

Today, Little Louie's
nose was clogged.

His ears crackled

and his brain felt full.
(He didn't know of what.)

But mostly, his nose.
It was disgusting.

Little Louie didn't want to color.

Or watch TV.

He didn't even want to shoot baskets with wadded-up tissues.
All he wanted (besides maybe some hot chocolate) was his mother.

 called Little Louie with his weird,
all-wrong, stuffed-up voice.

His dog, Bob, came running. And slobbering.

NO!
I wan by
BOB,
not
BOB!
BOB! BOB! BOB!

Bob didn't know what to say to that.

Little Louie's mother came to his bedroom door.
"Why all the yelling, Punkin'?" asked Mom.
Little Louie let out a sad
I-don't-feel-well-and-my-nose-is-clogged moan.

Uhhhhhh

"Okay, Sweetie. Let's see . . ."
It didn't matter what she was going to say—
all Little Louie wanted was his mom.
But she had to get his sister from the bus.

The next day, Little Louie was even sicker.
His lips chapped and his eyes gunked.
As for his nose, you can't even imagine.

So he just lay there getting hot and sweaty,
which sounded like "Hotten Smetty."
"Who's Hotten Smetty?" asked his sister.

No. Not SMETTY. SMEDDY! And HODD!

Tessa didn't know who Smeddy was. Hodd either.

Mom would understand.

BOB! called Little Louie.

His dog, Bob, came running. And slobbering.

Tessa looked at him like he was cuckoo. So did Bob.

Little Louie was starting to feel kind of cuckoo,
and nothing seemed to help.

I doan wan
by bedicine.
I doan wanda
bubba bat.
And I doan
wanda dap.*

*(I don't want my medicine.
I don't want a bubble bath.
And I don't want a nap.)

I just wan by BOB!

Bob came running. And slobbering.

Little Louie was all mixed up.

So was Bob.

So was Mom.

She dropped the laundry and kicked off her shoes.

She climbed in next to Little Louie and pulled the blankets high. She held him close. "Oh, Louie," she said.

Oh, Bob... he said.

Bob came running. And slobbering.

He jumped up on the bed with them,
and they lay there all afternoon,
cozy as could be.

And even though Little Louie wasn't all that little,
and didn't need his mother every minute of the day,
well, it was still awfully nice to have her there.

Bob, too.

Little by little, Louie got better.

His nose un-clogged.

His ears un-crackled.

And when he yelled **BOB!** it was because he actually wanted Bob!

Bob came running. And jumping. And slobbering.

And even though Little Louie didn't actually
need his mom every minute of the day,
he thought it was awfully nice when she came running too.

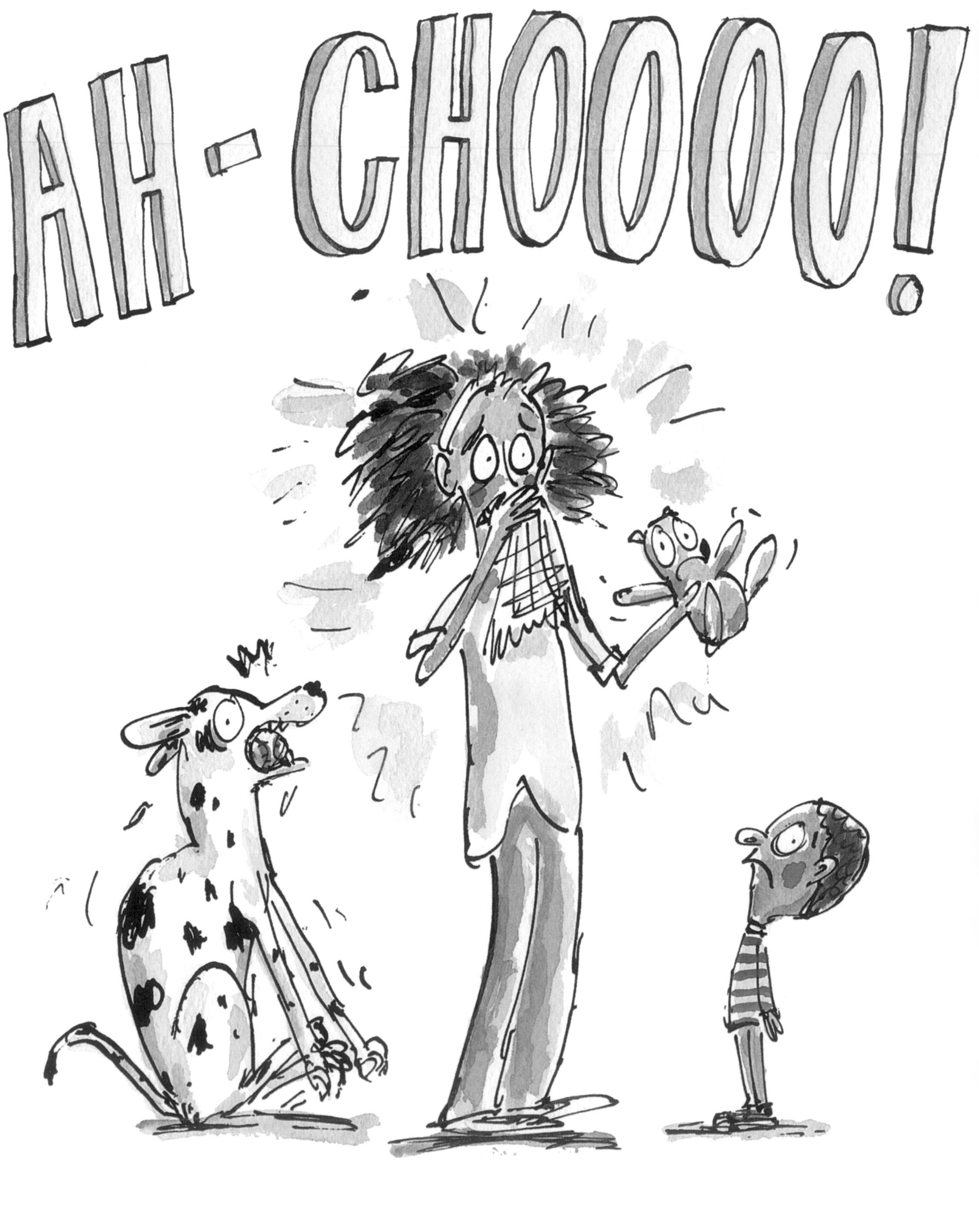
AH-CHOOOO!